I Bought a Baby Chicken

by Kelly Milner Halls   Illustrated by Karen Stormer Brooks

Boyds Mills Press

Published by Caroline House
Boyds Mills Press, Inc.
A Highlights Company
815 Church Street
Honesdale, Pennsylvania 18431
Printed in China

Publisher Cataloging-in-Publication Data
Halls, Kelly Milner.
I Bought a Baby Chicken / by Kelly Milner Halls ;
illustrated by Karen Stormer Brooks.-1st ed.
[32]p. : col. ill. ;   cm.
Summary: When a girl buys a baby chicken, her family buys lots of chicks,
too, in this rhyming picture book.
ISBN 1-56397-800-8
1. Chickens -- Fiction -- Juvenile literature. 2. Stories in rhyme--
Juvenile literature. 3. Counting-out rhymes. 4. Counting--Fiction
--Juvenile literature. [1. Chickens--Fiction. 2. Stories in rhyme.
3. Counting-out rhymes. 4. Counting--Fiction.] I. Brooks, Karen
Stormer, ill. II. Title.
[E] -dc21   2000   AC   CIP
99-62642

First edition, 2000
The text of this book is set in 39-point Rotis Semisans.

10 9 8 7 6 5 4 3 2 1

Baby Chicken is dedicated to my two daughters, Kerry and Vanessa, who inspire
and delight me each and every day (and who really did have pet chickens);
to my parents, Gene and Georgia Milner; and to my sister Kim. I love them more than life itself.
It is also dedicated to one of my oldest friends,
Rick Spears, who helped make this collaboration possible and
kept me steady even before the path was clear. Thanks!

—K. M. H.

For Connor and Holly, and especially Scott—
who helped me count these chicks before they were hatched.

—K. S. B.

I bought
a baby chicken
at the general store.

My sister liked
the black ones,
so she gathered up
two more.

My father spied
the striped ones,
so he picked
a group of three.

And Mommy had
four red ones
when I turned
around to see.

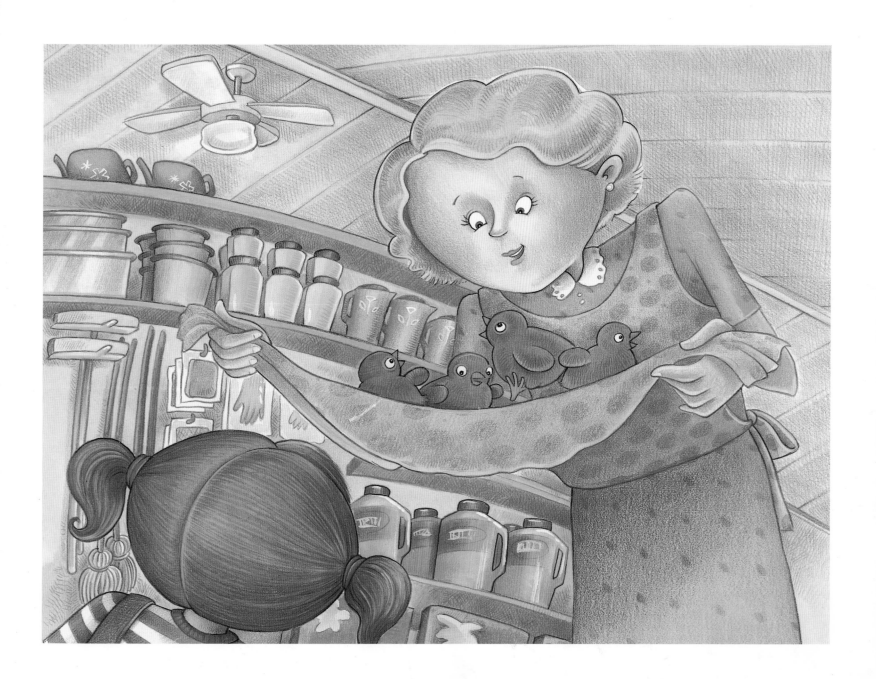

My cousin hollered,

"Gimme some!"

and
carried
five away.

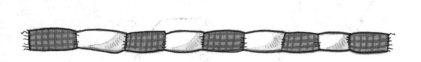

His sister got
six white ones
'cause she had
to have her way.

My grammy
smooched a
brown chick
and promptly
gathered seven.

Old Grandpa
scooted out eight
as the cashier cried,
"My heavens!"

Great-granny
boxed up
her supply, which
added up to nine.

Great-grandpa
picked out ten
and stepped into
the checkout line.

When all the dust
had settled, we had more
than fifty head.

There were chickens
in the kitchen . . .

. . . There were chickens
in my bed!

There were baby chicks
most everywhere,
as you must know by now . . .

I guess my family's lucky
that I didn't want a cow!